Maev Barba

Presents

Issue 1

Maev Barba Presents
Published by Pluto House
www.plutohouse.space

Copyright © 2023 by Maev Barba
ISBN: 9781949127256

Cover art by Lucas on Fiverr
@bobsokova

Maev Barba Presents

Le décapité parlant. Artist: C. Gilbert.

From *Popular scientific recreations in natural philosophy, astronomy, geology, chemistry.* London: Ward, Lock, and Co., n.d. [ca. 1882].

For Harley.

A Note from the Formatter

These first ten issues (the remaining nine to be published throughout 2023) were primarily formatted at Yaboo Café and This Café in Taipei, Taiwan, and later at ReEcho Coffee and Ink Café in Hsinchu, Taiwan.

This Café: zhejiancafe
No. 39, Lane 30, Section 4, Xinyi Rd, Da'an District, Taipei City, 106

ReEcho Coffee: reecho_coffee
No. 8, Lane 58, Minsheng Rd, East District, Hsinchu City, 30043

Ink Café: inkcafe
No. 180, Linsen Rd, East District, Hsinchu City, 300

Thank you very much to the kind people at these cafes for providing such beautiful spaces and unparalleled coffee.

A Letter from the Editor

We have started our small community. You are welcome to come. We have sequestered away in the woods of Vashon Island. For those interested in joining, we invite you, arms open. It is only a short distance to Vashon Island but a world of difference. We will find our muses at any cost.

Deep in the woods of Bainbridge Island, floating in Puget Sound, we are building a new observatory.

We all know what an observatory is, but here are a few definitions from Cambridge: "1. a place where stars, planets, and other celestial bodies are observed, usually through a telescope; also, a place for observing meteorological or other natural phenomena. 2. A lookout (vantage point with a view of the surrounding area). 3. A situation or structure commanding a wide view."

What many consider the world's first observatory, as we consider the definition and function of an observatory today, was built by Hipparchus, the "father of astronomy," on the island of Rhodes around 150 BCE.

Hipparchus discovered the precession of the equinoxes, a gradual gravity-induced shift in Earth's axis, known more precisely today as general precession. Through observations in his observatory, he created a map to the stars. The map is lost and still searched for today.

There are many observatories and proto-observatories throughout history. Stonehenge, built sometime between 3000 and 1520 BCE in Wiltshire, England, tracks the position of the Sun, Moon, and stars. Even older is Newgrange in County Meath, Ireland. Estimated construction at 3150 BC, Newgrange likely predates Stonehenge a thousand years.

Newgrange is a massive grass-covered dome 35m in diameter. Newgrange is a passage tomb, a kind of labyrinthine gravesite and temple, which used to admit winter solstice light in through a hole in the stone above the entrance. Today, sunlight shines through the gap at 4.5 minutes after sunrise, whereas 5,000 years ago, sunlight would have entered the precise moment the sun peered over the horizon (the moon's gravitational pull has altered the Earth's incline in relation to the sun by 23.5 degrees—the precession of the equinoxes).

The priests of Babylonia also measured celestial movement from the mud of their ziggurats and recorded on clay tablets the first written observation of Hailey's comet. I enjoy imagining this: a handful of philosophers running to the top of the ziggurat as the black sky rent by fire, Hayley's beautiful tail.

In the dark and thorough forests of Puget Sound's Bainbridge Island, we build our humble structure, and one day from this structure, we will observe the stars more intimately than ever before.

Hegel and Heine wandered into the night and looked at the sky. Heine marveled that the night sky, full of gleaming stars, was the "abode of the blessed." Hegel said it was "only a gleaming leprosy in the sky."

Hegel said this because he believed the concrete higher than the abstract. Will, progress, striving—these are what count. Stars do not strive. They are a chemical process, a division of helium into hydrogen. They have no will. They will split and explode.

Are stars inferior?

What is so special about the 'concrete' (human endeavor, for Hegel) if its awareness of itself is all that separates it from the exploding Sun?

Let us transition to this fact. Namely, this book is all fiction. What do we privilege, the author's life or work? How does the author use a life? Do they turn into drama?

If one considers life the mere source material for drama, then may all be permitted. One may murder, rape, and cheat in the book's name. It does not matter if you are in jail or otherwise confined; all that matters is that you are writing your evils onto paper.

I tell myself this often: *put me in jail; I don't want society; I want to write.* To the poet, all, and all to *excess*, is permitted, encouraged, perverted. How dangerous is this?

I am the cause of many great and terrible evils. And what of Eric, or Bob, or Arnold, or Ben? Have they not also murdered or cheated or lied?

There is no redemption in writing about it. Instead, we are building, of stone and mud and concrete, the observatory. By forming something with our hands, not merely describing it, but by *building* it, we are building our road to the stars.

Every day coming together as a group, building our walls, and digging up, we create our greatest mode of observance: dirtying our bodies and soaking in sweat. We have no powered equipment. We dig early in the morning and late into the night.

We have chosen a location in the Bainbridge woods where the trees have grown strangely and incredibly thick, which cannot be viewed from outside but must be found through a winding, twisting, and tightening walk through the woods. It is easy to lose one's way. One must be focused and not deviate, ever turning, winding, twisting round the path like a thread wrapped around a spool.

While the astronomical costs of specific scientific equipment are concrete barriers, we hope that through selling these process pieces, or sketches and progress in these pages, in this series of fiction, *Maev Barba Presents*, we may gradually purchase the necessary lenses, astrolabes, and mirrors and thereby day by day pull ourselves from up from the mud and into the stars.

The best stories in *Maev Barba Presents* were originally published in Deep Overstock. Thank you to Mickey Collins and his editors for permitting us to use these stories in *MBP*. Deep Overstock, the international booksellers' journal, accepts fiction year-round.

Visit the DO website for more information: **www.deepoverstock.com**

The lover of great stories looks in the book and considers neither the small as too little nor the large as too great, for the great lover of stories knows there is no limit to dimension.

MOTHER DOME

Maev Barba

As my mother is equally afraid of small spaces as she is of large spaces, I will build my mother a geodesic dome, its outer wall comprised of two walls, essentially a dome over a dome, with three feet of space between the two domes. The dome is then a very large space comprising many small spaces. Because a geodesic dome is made up of many triangles and because—if the two domes are three feet apart—we may put narrow landings in every triangle so that the inhabitant, or visitor, might sit, rest, or hide in any one of the many triangles.

I am about six feet tall but bent in half, I fit in any triangle with three sides of three feet (area: 3.9 feet).

To make the geodesic dome, rows of slightly smaller triangles are arranged upon slightly larger triangles which are arranged below slightly smaller triangles, and on and on until the pattern forms a dome (this is oversimplified, of course; in reality, the larger triangles form pentagons and the smaller triangles form hexagons and the dome is formed by rows of pentagons followed by rows of hexagons, and so on; but this does not change the fact that we're looking at triangles).

If my mother can reach up to feel with her hands something up to seven feet tall, then my mother will be able to reach up and feel around from any bottommost triangle to any second bottommost triangle. If I provide her with a stick three feet in length, she will be able to poke around in any third-level triangle.

Now, if it took my mother ten seconds to, in total darkness, determine whether or not I was inside any given triangle, and if my mother went about this systematically (not wildly running triangle to triangle wherever her fear compels her, screaming and calling for me) checking triangle after triangle, it would take her thirty seconds to check each column, bottom-most triangle to topmost triangle.

My mother could then, within reason–at ten seconds per triangle, three triangles per column–examine two columns per minute or one hundred and twenty columns an hour. Given that this is the Pacific Northwest and at this time of year, we have roughly eight hours every night of total darkness, I believe my mother could (again, if she is rational and efficient) examine nine hundred and sixty triangles per night.

Three rules I will follow:

1. I will never hide in any triangle which my mother cannot reach.

2. I will never switch triangles at any point in the night. When darkness falls and I enter the dome, I pick one triangle and stay in it.

3. On any given night, I may enter the dome from any direction and climb into any triangle, so long as I don't violate rules one or two.

On any given night, my mother's odds of finding me are dependent totally on the size of the dome. Given a dome with a diameter of one hundred feet and a height of fifty feet, and therefore with the dome surface area of 15,707.96 feet, we divide 15,707.96 feet by the area of one triangle, so 15,707.96 feet divided by 3.9 feet, equaling 4027.68, rounding up to 4028 total triangles.

Given that my mother is only capable of searching the first three triangles in any given column, and given the diminishing number of triangles (a loss of six per hexagon every row moving up–the largest number at the bottom of the dome and the smallest number, being the dome's topmost point, one hexagon at the top), row-by-row, a dome with 4028 triangles, as my mother would only be capable of searching roughly ten percent (402 triangles) of the surface area of a dome fifty feet high (at 120 triangles examined per hour), it would take my mother less than half a night to examine every triangle in all three bottommost rows of the dome. Inevitably, she would find me.

Now, if we doubled the height and diameter of the dome (so, d=200 feet, h=100 feet) to get a dome surface area of 62,831.85, we then get 16,110.73 or, rounding up, 16,111 triangles. Searchability is diminished to seven percent because the dome is higher. My mother then can search 805 triangles. Again, piece of cake for my mother.

But if I design a dome one-thousand feet in diameter and five-hundred feet in height (dome surface area: 1,570,796.33 feet), then my mother must contend with 402,768 total triangles, five thousand searchable triangles, her chances of finding me in one night are reduced to roughly one night in five nights.

And a dome of one-hundred thousand feet in diameter and fifty-thousand feet in height (dome surface area: 15,707,963,267.95 feet)? My mother has an estimated 5,034,604 searchable triangles. A dome of 5,034,604 searchable triangles has a total volume of 261,799,387,799,149.4 cubic feet, the same volume as if Lake Michigan flooded Lake Huron.

In a dome of this size, my mother, on any given night, has a 1 in 5594 chance of finding me. If she spends every night systematically examining triangles (maintaining her rate of 960 triangles examined per night), feeling around in every triangle in the dark, and poking at the upper triangles with a stick, I will see my mother only once every fifteen years.

Rond de serviette soulevé par un rapide mouvement de rotation. — *Force centrifuge et résistance de frottement.* "An illustration of centrifugal force." Engraver: Louis Poyet. Caption taken from the English edition titled *Popular scientific recreations in natural philosophy, astronomy, geology, chemistry.* London: Ward, Lock, and Co., n.d. [ca. 1882].

FRIENDSHIP 7

Robert Eversmann

Mothers love astronauts. Mother salute their boys and button their astronaut shirts. These astronaut boys choosing these hard vacuums of space! These boys choosing beyond any reaches or limits!

"Space camp" is a lie. There is no "space camp." There is only the abandoned rotten-walled house with a cellar full of mirrors. These boys who lied about "anti-gravity," about "human centrifuges," about "the space-time continuum," who lied just to steal their mothers' jewelry. To take it, wear it—clasp it around their necks, wrists, fingers, gilded, jeweled—down into. the cellar, down to see themselves shining like diamonds in mirrors. They traded gold between them like pirates and held earrings to their ears before the mirrors. "We're rich," they said.

But "Hey," said one boy. "I have something even better." He had been waiting for this moment. He lifted his shirt. There was something in his stomach; his belly distended. Something was wrong. He looked like a snake who had eaten a bicycle. He claimed that inside his stomach was the tail fin of a rocket.

The other boys gathered around to touch it and ran their fingers up its contours.

"It's something all right," said one boy.

"It's no spaceship," said another.

"Feel it," said one.

"No. I won't feel it," said another.

But the boy with the spaceship in his stomach took the other boy's finger and brought it to his scar. His stomach was rigid like a rocket fin and strained like the rocket might split through his skin.

"Well," said the one boy. He moved the fin a little left, a little right. "Does that hurt?"

The boy with the spaceship sat up on his elbows. "No, it doesn't hurt," he said.

"What if we take it out of you?" said one. He grabbed the fin with his spider fingers and tugged. "Would that hurt?"

"No. Maybe. I don't think so," he said. He flicked the ridge in his stomach, inside a ringing clang.

Another said, "Let's tear it out and ride him to space."

The boys laughed at first, but in mentioning "space," they remembered their mothers. "Space camp! Space camp!" Their mothers had been so excited — little liars.

The metal thing suddenly clunked on its own. The boys removed their hands. The thing in the boy's stomach had pointed distinctly to the left. It clunked a second time the other way, and his belly button swelled—a sound like a backfiring car. The boys stood back.

The scar split open, the skin separated, and the stomach gaped.

The wound spread like a spill. It widened and then spun like a spiral of sugar until finally turning black and empty like infinite space.

"Wo," said the boys. They couldn't see to the other side. It was just a hole that stretched on for light years, a black hole of nothingness.

Light things drifted toward the black hole, dust from the basement, and the uneaten peanuts from one boy's box of crackerjacks. The boys came closer, and their hair was sucked toward the stomach.

The boy yanked down his shirt, which sucked in like a dent. "Hey!" he protested.

The boys felt around the edge of the hole with their fingers, and their fingers stretched like long beams of light. The boy with the crackerjacks disappeared his arm to his shoulder but couldn't reclaim any of his peanuts.

What unfolded before them weighed heavily on their souls. Oh, how the boys regretted deceiving their mothers.

"What have we done? What kind of astronaut throws his mother's love away? We're hardly astronauts at all," they decided, and all spit on the ground. "Are we monsters?" They crossed their arms and paced.

But then it came to them. The boys had an idea. The solution was clear.

"We can't keep it," they said. "We're afraid of what we've done."

"No," said the boy.

"But we're your friends," they said. The boys gathered their jewelry in their hands. They approached the boy like merchants.

"No, please."

"But look at what you've done to us. We couldn't have done this ourselves. We aren't those kinds of boys. But you…"

The boys pointed at the boy with the black hole.

"I know a guilty boy when I see one. And you are it."

They held him down and emptied their hands
into him: their fake gold rings, fake rubies, fake
pearls–what boys, betraying their mothers–fake
pearl-inlay crane hairpins and duo pendants–
what boys, betraying their mothers only signs of
love left–sterling silver and rose gold Fabergé
egg, two of them, strung by a double-wound
gold chain, sterling circlets, one with a pearl
clasp, one with a ruby, one a Scottish Terrier
brooch with rubies for eyes, and the single white
gold choker in the style of the Whitecleuch Chain.

Six empty boys like a thousand in a cellar full
of mirrors. Six shivering boys ashamed like dogs,
skinny ones. And the one boy there alone,
shunned in the corner, disappearing and
reappearing his hand into the black hole. Clouds
of dust picked up and circled him.

"We wouldn't have done it if it weren't for
him," said one boy. "I've never stolen anything.
I don't even like jewelry."

"Yes. He has spoiled us," said another.
"Pushed evil into our hands." He cringed into his
own hands. "We aren't to blame."

"Tuck his head into his chest," said a third.
"Let his black hole swallow him!" He pushed the
boy by his neck and began to close inward like a
crab being boiled.

"No," said the first boy, Sam, who was a natural leader. He wore Nikes and a tracksuit. "If he is gone," he said, "then we will be blamed. This, as I see it, is an opportunity. Have any of you been through a black hole before?"

As the boy with the black hole held his head in his hand and lamented what he had become, the other boys looked at each other's faces, all uncertain. No boy had been through a black hole.

"I nominate you, Pete," Sam said.

Pete was the ashen boy, white like clear sap. His hands were sticky from licking crackerjack residue from his fingers. "Me?" he said, pulling his finger from his mouth.

"Yes, Pete," said Sam. The other boys stood back and watched. "Look at you."

Pete looked at himself. He was also shorter than the other boys. His arms were too long, and his eyes were two different browns.

"You're a natural explorer," said Sam.

"Yes," the other boys agreed. "It's true. You're our best shot." The boys held the boy with the black hole down. They pulled up his shirt. The black hole churned like ice cream mixed by a machine. Pete gulped. For some reason, he took his shoes off. The other boys furrowed their brows.

"I don't know," said the boy with the black hole.

Pete's eyes were as clear as a jam jar of water. He bent to the black hole. "What happens if I don't come back?" he said.

"It's for science, Pete," said Sam.

Pete sighed and put his head in the black hole.

He might have said something like, *wow* or *amazing,* but no one heard him because he said it into a black hole. The only sound was the boy's whimpering with a cosmic anomaly gaping in the center of his chest.

"What do you see, Pete?" they said.

No response.

They looked each other over. They looked at Sam. Sam nodded. They lifted Pete by the ankles and, though they struggled as he kicked, held Pete there, apparently headless, suspended above the black hole.

Sam circled the scene. It was like a group of fishermen with an alien marlin. When the boys had steadied their ground, they looked at Sam. Sam looked at the ground but nodded.

They lowered Pete to his shoulders, elbows, and waist until it was as if they were holding two detached legs, then they dropped him, and Pete slipped away inside the black hole.

There was no sign of him except for the shoes he had left behind. They stood over where they had dropped their friend. It was as if they had pushed him into a well.

"What have I done?" said the boy with the black hole in a tiny, terrible voice, staring at the hole in his stomach.

Sam rocked on his heels. "This is an unprecedented event," he said. He stared at the ceiling, which, as they were in the basement, was just the threshold before the first floor. He looked again at the situation, then messily pointed at the other boys. "Ok," he said.

The boys forced their way inside. It looked like a playful wrestle, but over time, each boy disappeared.

Now there was no one left but the boy with the black hole. He considered putting his hands inside and seeing if he really would collapse, but as he lifted his hands to his stomach, the black closed and the boy's stomach again into the skin, leaving only a little scar.

The boy went through life explaining himself. He couldn't believe he still existed. He was the last one to have seen them.

He told everyone he was the cause of everything. He had done it all, all the evil in the world. No one believed him, of course. People only felt sorry for him. He was a boy who had lost all his friends in one go. How else was he to feel?

He bumped his head against the wall to bruise it, at home and at school, *bump, bump, bump, bump, bump*, and he deliberately burned himself, pushed his fingers on anything hot, told his teachers that he was the scum of the earth, and didn't deserve Christmas, told his parents, as they were slicing his twelfth birthday cake, that he better not wake up tomorrow, that that cake had better be poisoned, and told the police, whenever he saw them on the street or whenever they visited his school, saying they'd better come shoot him, they'd better come shoot him because he'd made his friends disappear. But they only gave him a junior officer sticker and told him he was good.

A year passed, and the ridge of a spaceship formed in his stomach again. He sat poking it in his room. His mother came in.

"Another spaceship?" she said. He took a long time to respond to anything anyone asked him. "I baked you some cookies," she said.

They were rocket-shaped, and she'd iced them with sayings like "Challenger" and "Houston" and "It's not your fault."

She set the plate of cookies on his bed and smoothed his hair. He didn't like hearing anything about himself, so when she left, he ate some of an "It's not your fault" cookie and traced the scar up his stomach, which opened, split, separated, then expanded and forced him to lie flat on his back. Six grown men stepped out of his chest and into his room.

"What a wild forty-five years," said one.

"Time sneaks up on you," said another.

Some were gray in the face. Some had beards. Some were muscular, and some were fat. Three of them wore baseball caps.

The boy hugged each of them, crying. He was so happy. "Do you want to play?" he said.

They took their share of cookies but said, "No, I suspect we'd better up and find work," said one.

"Get wives," said another. "And get some kids of our own. Make them do the playing. And us the relaxing."

"Haha," they laughed.

They'd been through so much in that other dimension. But now it was time to settle down. Build a house. Put down roots. Get to know their neighbors. It took crossing space to get through their childhoods. The boy, who sat alone in his bedroom, would have to get through his too. He was a child, and he had missed his friends' lives.

Les trains de projectiles pour la lune. "Projectile trains for the moon." Artist: Henri de Montaut. Engraver: Adolphe François Pannemaker. From From the Earth to the Moon by Jules Verne.

THE WHALE

Eric Thralby

Then Jonah prayed to the LORD his God from the belly of the fish, saying, "I called out to the LORD, out of my distress, and he answered me; out of the belly of Sheol I cried, and you heard my voice. For you cast me into the deep, into the heart of the seas, and the flood surrounded me; all your waves and your billows passed over me. Then I said, 'I am driven away from your sight; yet I shall again look upon your holy temple.' The waters closed over me to take my life; the deep surrounded me; weeds were wrapped about my head ...

—Jonah 2:1-10

Near nightfall, we hammered a pack of Piccolo Petes, then went to the dunes.

We found a depression in the dunes with very steep sides. We slid to the bottom, lit the Petes, then scrambled back up.

The bang stuck in my ears. I poked my fingers inside, but it was like two rocks had been shoved to the back. We judged it a success by the mass of blackness in the sand and the smoke rising between us. The jagged and gaping duct tape shell was now six times its original size, violent and huge.

Bob said something to me. I read his lips. *Fuck,* I think he said, but I couldn't hear. My jaw ached. My teeth ached. "*Fuck,*" I said. And this time, I hear a sharp ring coming swiftly behind it. *That was awesome*. I could almost hear him. And now there was even a growing rush of wind about me. I was deaf, but something—something as if leaping onto the back of that deafness, a new sound spilled from the sound dunes about us, laborious and mammoth like the displacement of waves, as if an immense underwater ship had suddenly surfaced. Bob and I abandoned the Petes and slipped our way back to the top.

A shadow grew, something inside the water like a geological form. As it began to emerge, it gave the impression of an avalanche caught on film and the tape run backward, the succession of cliff face after cliff face leaping one over the other, a crowd of people in escape, these waves which formed and tumbled. It was as if Haystack Rock had tipped, rolled, and come straight forward, a harrowing mountain bounding for shore until finally, we saw plunge upward from the deep: the black-grey figure, like an oil tanker wrapped in skin, longer than a gasoline truck, and about three times as thick: a whale.

The moon shined deeply into the whale. The whale drew in closer, yet incapable of escape. We could tell now it was not visiting but struggling.

The adults, emerging from their dark forested houses and spreading down the hill, identified it as a sperm whale. They held their robes and shined their flashlights at the whale. They stepped into the waves up to their ankles.

Half-concealed in water and wave, the whale was still larger than the crowd of our town's entire population. A few adults drove boats out to tie and tow the whale, but the closer they got, the more agitated the whale became, pulling and straining, splitting waves with its tail, cracking like thunder.

Something tensed at its mouth, then—a great and sudden *tick*. Dozens of us fell or hobbled backward, pushing our hands to our ears. A second great *tick* and I fell flat into the waves. It was like a bomb had gone off—even more blunt trauma to my ears. Still, I could hear, but there the high-pitched ringing had returned. I stumbled through the waves, rubbing at my face, pressing between my neck and jaw to reestablish some normalcy into my ears. (Sperm whales, like dolphins, click like to communicate with one another. Only sperm whales can click at a 'gunshot' volume of up to 230 decibels, so loud that the sound waves can make a human body explode.)

Desperate, our community dove into the waves and pushed barehanded on the whale. Through the crashing whoosh of deafness and whale, I heard the cries of the adults, desperate and raging, evidently no longer just in the spirit of saving an animal but now as if against futility itself. In pushing the whale, it felt as if we pushed against our lives, whether trying to right or push them away. Three hours of this and the whale finally went still. The whale's last few clicks, though explosive and guttural like massive dry ice bombs buried in sand, became slow, deliberate, and finally tired.

The whale lay still. The waves, which had lapped at its eyes and near its crown, had receded, taking the water away like a net.

The whale's eye, massive and lopsided, seemed to watch us. It looked almost dented as if it were too heavy to be perfectly round.

Bob and I came around to the front and looked in. The mouth reeked of briny sea and fish. I rubbed my hand against its skin.

"No," said a man. He stepped forward but did nothing to stop me. Its skin. Something unfathomable. An ache of something so deep from the ocean. It had gone to the darkest places on Earth, this immense gaping mouth swallowing, gulping, devouring all it wanted.

New anxiety grew in the adults as they, having failed, stood, and shivered in darkness. Here was a sign: the most enormous imaginable corpse. A tower looming. A mountain of perishing flesh. The heat in their bodies as they had pushed in the whales had now frozen. They stood there with their arms stiff. This corpse — it marked them. They had to reject it.

The adults pushed us away and whispered to themselves. They rubbed their arms. They touched each other. They did not know what to do. They had tried to be rid of it. Now, here it was, here to stay.

Bob and I approached the whale's mouth. A sperm whale's mouth is disturbing. It is the exact height and width of an exceptionally tall and grotesquely thin man. It has teeth only on its bottom jaw and sockets in its upper jaw, which act like sheathes for the teeth. As narrow as it is long, the sperm whale's bottom jaw is like a section of floorboard struck through with candle-shaped nails. The teeth are so long they would pierce through your chest and come out your back. Closed, the sperm whale's mouth resembles the nearly seamless, unnoticeable attic door of any American house from which a washer dangles, tied up in string, ready to be pulled and peeled from the ceiling, unfolding a hidden ladder.

A wave hit me and shifted the whale. The water had already gone out so much with the tide that I hadn't expected it and lost my grip. Bob caught me by the shoulder.

The waves swept away from our ankles as we felt our hands about its mouth. It was like feeling inside a crack in stone. It became wet and pliable. I felt for its gums. Finding a weaker pocket near the back of its jaw, a fold in its lip, I slipped my hand in. I reached further, straining up to my shoulder. The smell of deep ocean became overwhelming.

"Do you feel anything?" said Bob. "Is there anything inside?"

I reached further into its mouth. I felt something. For a moment, I thought it was a hand.

"Help," I said. I slid backward. "Help."

Bob pushed on my back. We repositioned, lying down, and bracing ourselves against the sand. I pushed both arms back inside. I gripped it tightly now. We pulled. It would not budge. Again, something shifted about the whale. As we held on, a second sneaker wave slipped out from under the whale we sank underwater up to our necks.

"It's falling," I said.

The whale continued to shift. I choked up on the hand and clasped my fingers around a wrist. New waves again crashed above our heads like the morning, and the tide was coming. Water covered my nose, and I held my breath. It was as if we were trapped in a car that had flown from the bridge. I could not breathe. The water danced over my eyes.

I gasped for air and inhaled water. I had no choice. I let go completely, and, like a trapdoor, the whale's mouth snapped suddenly shut.

Bob pulled me up. I spit up what I swallowed and breathed. The whale's closed mouth was entirely underwater now. The tide had indeed come in. The ocean had choked up on the beach.

Though covered slightly by the tied, the whale lay there as prominent as ever.

Something drifted from the waves, a stick, or a board. It idled in the waves like a twig in a stream, passing by several men who only, motionless, not daring to touch it, peered gravely down as it drifted slowly passed them.

Finally, Courtney Man, the owner of Captain's Quarters, a gentlemen's club, took up the board. This got people's attention. People trusted the personality of Courtney Man. The crowd knit tightly around him.

He stood in the waves rubbing the board with the heel of his hand. He dropped it back into the ocean. A chill had split through him, and he had turned white as smoke.

"What is it, Courtney?" said a man close behind him. "What does it say?"

Courtney turned around. When finally, he faced us, his eyes beads and his lips blue and trembling, he said: "The Cabinet of Children."

A wave passed through the crowd of adults, and they collectively stumbled.

"But go there, lonely, / At eventide, / And hearken, hearken / To the lisping tide." Artist: Thomas Dalziel.

From *Ballad Stories of the Affections* by Robert Williams Buchanan. London: George Routledge and Sons [n.d.]

The following day was devoted to discussing how to dispose of the whale. Rancid smells of the bottom of the ocean had already infested every bedroom and would only compound with time. We could not afford to have the whale towed away.

By nighttime, after a whole day of debate around the bonfires near the whale, we came to a collective and final decision: the next morning, two days after the arrival of the whale, we would fill its mouth with dynamite, lead a fuse far away into the dunes, or even into the neighborhoods, and then we would detonate the whale.

People looked dreamily at their hands. They had failed the whale, and now they would explode it.

Courtney Man stepped out from the crowd and stood before the mouth of the whale. He regarded the whale. It was so massive that it cast us in definite shadow, even in the moon's dim light.

"You may take this as an omen," Courtney said, but then he looked into the sky and flinched.

He paced around the group and peered at individual faces, fluttering with light from the bonfires in darkness as if each face were shapeshifting. "I say," he said, "that all which has entered the whale, all that it has eaten, and all that we have hidden, will be finally erased in the morning for good."

That night, the night before detonation, Bob and I prepared flashlights.

We left at about midnight from Bob's house and came down the hill to the beach. All the houses were dark. Everyone, so we thought, must still have been exhausted from the events of the whale and were all still in bed, sound asleep.

When we arrived at the ocean, the tide had left, and the waves merely lapped at the nose of the whale.

When I shined my flashlight at its mouth, I saw something strange in the sand.

"What the fuck?" Bob said.

It was a pile of clothing. We looked behind us and around us. There was nothing but the sound of waves.

I picked up a pair of blue jeans by the belt. "They must be from earlier," I said. "Maybe some of them took off their clothes if they had swimsuits underneath, and then they just forgot them."

I dropped the jeans back down and shined my flashlight at a discrepancy I noticed in the whale's mouth.

"Bob," I said. "Do you see that?"

I pinpointed the light at a spot where the whale's upper and lower jaw looked pushed apart.

Bob got closer. I reached in. "It's missing teeth," I said. I sat down in the sand and pulled down on its lower jaw.

"No," he said. He shined his light in its gleaming teeth. "They've been cut."

I ran my fingers through the gap and found half a dozen jagged nubs were cut down to the surface of its jaw. As we pushed up against its upper lip, we found a space big enough almost for a human to crawl through. We shined our lights inside and tried to see what we could see.

"Can whales eat people?" I said.

"I guess," he said. "I mean, they could. They're big enough, I mean."

I shined my light from left to right in an arc, seeing what seemed like ridges in the side of a tongue, then straight back into its cavernous throat. Bending the light upwards, I could see ribs like supports in a mining tunnel.

"*Fuck*," said Bob. He dropped his light. It slipped into the whale's mouth. Bob sat in the sand. "What the fuck," he said. He was breathing like he'd been chased.

I looked back into the whale. I twisted my light around inside, but still, I couldn't see anything that warranted such a reaction. Perhaps it was only unsettling the nature of the sperm whale's cave-like throat, so dark and strange, like a door into a terrible world.

There was a sudden vibration.

Bob and I looked at each other.

It was like the vibration of a machine, yet sloppy and wet as if something was churning, processing, inside the whale.

"It's the whale's digestion," I said. "It can. It still digests after death. It's such a big animal."

I put my ear against the whale.

"Shh," I said. There was something inside. It was so faint it was like someone crying in the bottom of a well.

"Someone's inside," I said.

But the voice changed in pitch. What had been the voice of a young woman was lowering,

lowering, and morphed into the voice of a man, then men, then —

"It's not one person," I said.

I followed the sound down the whale's tail, keeping my ear against its flesh, and found that the sounds grew nearer its belly.

The first sound changed in character, or perhaps only our understanding of it changed; I pictured vast parts of a giant moving, operating, interlocking, and clanking; it was like a machine but made of fleshy wetness, squelching, and sucking. The whale's mouth began to split open. A light emerged from its smile.

Bob and I ran to a piece of driftwood nearby, big enough to conceal us both, then we stared from behind it at the mouth of the whale.

"What's happening?" I said.

"What's inside?" Bob said.

The whale's lips trembled as a human hand emerged. It flexed its fingers. It made circles with its wrist. A second hand emerged. Then the two together, reaching forward and making purchase in the sand. Finally, the hands pulled a body out. It slid out. A naked creature. A human adult, wet and glistening in the moonlight. As it stood upright, its heaping flesh made age clear to us:

this was a woman in her fifties or sixties. The long grey hair spilled back as it lifted its head. The woman, we realized, was our third-grade teacher: Mrs. Codder.

She leaned against the mouth of the whale, a few steps away from the pile of clothes, and squatted. We then heard the unmistakable sound of urination, pattering like hail to the sand. When she was finished, she went to the pile of clothes and pulled on a skirt. She was reaching for a blouse when some inexplicable sound emerged from Bob. Mrs. Codder suddenly paused, straightened up, and looked in our direction. She dropped the blouse back and crossed the sand swiftly as if still in a dream.

She stopped at the driftwood and stood over us. The sky was full of clouds and stars above her head. She saw us, eyes becoming open like the moon, the flashing reflection of fat light in her eyes as the moon shone opposite the ocean. She breathed heavily and spoke.

"I have found him," she said. "I have solved it. He is here." She reached for us, grasping for us, leaning over the driftwood. "He is here."

Bob and I sunk further into the sand.

"Look! I have done it!" she said. "Look. Look."

A second woman's voice came from the whale. A man's voice followed behind it. As Mrs. Codder turned around to regard them, three more hands emerged, squirming from the mouth of the whale. Bob and I ran.

"At the bottom of the sea." Artist: unknown.

From *Under the Waves; or, Diving in Deep Waters: A Tale* by Robert Michael Ballantyne. London: James Nisbet and Co. [1887]

The explosives experts, trailing the fuse in a long string behind them as we stuffed our ears with toilet paper and waited in our homes, exploded the whale at 11:14 AM, January 13, 1982. It took two-hundred units of dynamite.

It exploded into so many pieces that our whole town rained with blubber. Some of the pieces were so large that they crushed cars.

After that, the day passed in silence. The blubber remained. Stray dogs ate their fill of the bits of the whale scattered throughout.

Then the lines of cars began.

Where before all shops had been closed, they were now opened in haste, and like the birds which had gathered in concentric rings high above the whale, so had people streamed in from Portland and Olympia. Long lines of traffic lined our streets. Nothing like it had happened in almost a year. Never, not since the events of the Cabinet, had we seen any cars in our streets other than our own.

Whereas before, our town had been the pariah of the Pacific Northwest because of the events of the Cabinet. Nobody had dared come to our town until that deafening explosion. It had been like announcing a second gold rush, or as if the explosion were an invitation that woke them out of something and got them out of bed, they flocked to Long Beach. They gathered in our bars, shops, and streets to ask us about the whale, the explosion, and what it had all been like.

Still, we felt on edge. Would they ask us about the Cabinet? The disappearances? *How could you let something so terrible happen? Why didn't you stop it?* But all was forgotten, it seemed, or at least exploded and lost.

Highwaymen arrived to clean away the larger bits scavenger birds (initially scared off by the noise) eventually returned to finish off the rest of the blubber and meat, yet still, even seven days after, just wandering the streets, I could find blubber stuck in trees or plastered against chimneys, or even in mailboxes.

Once, on the way to the arcade, I thought I saw a wooden hand of fingers inside a pile of clear amber jell, but when I got on the ground and looked close, I found it was only a shadow in blubber. I backed away slowly, for when I stood up, I saw Mrs. Codder. She stood behind her fence and watched me with the jell.

This time, reality had crawled to us, naked and shining in the moonlight, squeezed from the belly of a whale, but Bob and I had managed nothing but to grasp at something inside a whale's mouth.

I have tried to talk about it with Bob. I sent him an early draft of this story, and he didn't respond. He has entirely left the whale out of his interpretation in *The Cabinet of Children*. The contention might be, I suppose, because only I touched it and, of the two of us, only I truly know what was really in the whale.

A Dive for Life. Artist: Unknown. From *Tales of Adventure in the Sea* by Robert Michael Ballantyne. London: James Nisbet [1875]

NIGHTMARE

Robert Eversmann

The cowboy built a small playground for the orphans. He had been an orphan until the train accident when he had taken up the black hat and revolver.

The orphans drifted around the brick perimeter.

As he held his arms out to celebrate the orphanage's completion, the orphans warmed the cowboy. He picked them up on his shoulders. He made them fly like airplanes.

The cowboy's bones grew brittle. The children pointed their fingers like guns.

The cowboy had a nightmare. The children were separating his body into parts and using them to build a horrible playground.

One orphan took a leg and installed it like one rung of the monkey bars.

One orphan took the cowboy's two arms, then popped off all seven fingers. He evenly spaced the rigid fingers on a captain's wheel suspended upon a safety pole above the bark chips. Land ho, he said, turning the wheel of fingers.

They hammered nails into the pieces of the cowboy, and the cowboy, integral to the playground, was spread evenly throughout it.

Finally, one orphan installed the cowboy's head above the entrance of the slide and yawned the cowboy's mouth open like a hatch: *Yeeeeeeeeeee haaaaaaaaaawwww…* it echoed like a mouth one-thousand feet underground.

All the cowboy has done to improve himself and his community — *don't you see what it has done?*

"He met the nightmare." Artist: Henry Opsovat. From *Shakespeare's Songs*. London: John Lane [1901]

DADS DIGGING HOLES

Robert Eversmann

Here we are, digging holes.

I've got mine. And you've got yours.

Aint it true.

I'm digging mine, well, because of my daughter. And you, your—

My only son.

After a sweat break, the two men set to work on their holes again. The one, the father of a son, took his winter coat off and threw it a little way away from the hole. The other, the father of a daughter, liked to overheat and kept his jacket on but removed his hat and gloves.

If they came to a rock, they dug it out, kept the rocks by his hole, and kept his clothes under his rocks.

My only son is cruel. I can't stand it. He kept poking his fingers in the cat's ears. The cat was dying, hissed, and could hardly move. I told him to stop, but every chance he got...

No, there's nothing worse than a daughter. You're cursed to want her and want her and want her. She gets all these little changes. And you want her even more. Want every inch of her.

By now, both coats were off. The man with the daughter in his flannel undershirt stained with sweat, and the man with the son, his shirt too drenched. Their holes now up to their noses. They had to shout to communicate.

Horrible, the father of a daughter. All I think, all day and all night, what if she comes in? What if she crawls into my bed? What will I do? The man pauses and stares over the handle end of his shovel.

Pity me, the father of a son, the father of a killer I've brought into the world.

A little water spilled onto each man's head. The tide rushed up and surprised them.

They got out from their holes and laid their shovels aside. The men yelled a few last things to each other and jumped into their separate holes, each man hunched in his hole with his rocks in his lap.

The waves came up as prettily as they do, filling the holes with water and sand.

Fauchelevent prit la pelle et Jean Valjean la pioche. "Fauchelevent took the shovel and Jean Valjean the pickaxe." Artist: Gustave Brion. From *Les Misérables* by Victor Hugo. Paris: J. Hetzel et A. Lacroix [1867]

DEAD HORSES

Robert Eversmann

We were about to throw tractor wheels when we found something better.

Doing anything with these dead horses, he asked. He had his little shorts, his name was Billy, and he walked like a man.

No, I said.

We dragged them out of the barn, maybe a dozen.

These are awkward and ungainly and truer to life, Billy said. Let's throw one as a marker to see if we improve.

He dragged one by the leg to a spot behind him, then dragged his toe in the dirt from his spot to mine.

This will be our throwing line, he said. He kissed his arm.

Can't stop sweating, I said. I laughed.

A bit of wind hit his hair as he hiked up his horse. I'll go first, he said.

His calves grew out as he balanced and shuffled his feet. He dug in, pumped his legs, and hurled it so it spun like a star, soaring and finally landing two solid body lengths away.

Two! Yeah! I yelled. Yeah!

He collapsed. I grabbed him up to bump chests, and we landed. Now it was my turn.

Ok, he said. He could barely speak. What you got. He slapped his legs and fell again. No chance, not a chance. Not against my horse.

I got down low and hiked it up on my shoulder.

A real pretty one with a white mane and a white belly like a seashell. I shuffled my legs underneath for a show.

Real heavy, I said.

He tossed some dirt at me. I got up. I pumped my legs and threw everything. High, strong arc, better than his. I fell back, and when I hit, it was still going. Finally, it came down. It bounced and then settled.

Ha! he yelled. A whole head shorter! A whole head! I beat you fair and square!

"My flesh trembleth for fear of thee; and I am afraid of thy judgments." —Psalm CXIX. 120.   Artist: Francis Quarles. From *Quarles' Emblems* by Francis Quarles. London: James Nisbet and Co. [1861]

MY FATHER, THE VILLAIN

Eric Thralby

My father was attacked by an unidentified animal. It concentrated on his eyes and neck. After this accident, my father became horrible to look at. What I mean is that my father has become a living, breathing threat.

When people look, he looks back. When people ask, he follows them into the store and harasses them until they leave. Our graduation rate plummets because children are terrified and refuse to go to school. Our mortality rate among the old skyrockets because of the safety in death.

We begin to worry he's become too aggressive, myself, my brother, and our two sisters and mother.

—

We buy him a mask and bring him to a mirror to try it on. We massage his shoulders, pat his arms, and encourage him with every sound we know. He stands as indifferent as a pile of rocks and pulls the mask on.

'What is it?' he says.

'It is a magical mask,' I say. 'It will instantly make you OK.'

He turns side to side, feeling the mask, looking close in the mirror as if shaving. Even under a magical mask, my father is as hideous as ever.

He pulls it off, walks past us, and leaves his mask on the counter.

I cannot say where he goes, but I can guess his usual haunts: the pet adoption center, any daycare within a radius, and, he has done it before, live television via the broadcasting tower.

———

The mask remains on the counter for weeks. Our father has become more and more, since the animal attack, a lump of putty, a pitiable man with always a handful of pebbles, and a heart full of hate. Whenever he stands up to leave, he stares us down until we recoil from his face. And then he slams the door and runs.

'But what will we do? Our mother has become a wreck and our father a plague.'

We sit on our couches and drink. I fumble the instructions, which I have taped back together, for the magical mask in my hands and read for my brother and sisters:

Welcome to the magical mask. If, indeed, the mask is no good, try encouraging words. Again, if this is to no effect, believe in the magic of gloves and a belt, among other accessories of choice. With love, from magic, the magical mask.

'This helps nothing,' says my sister, who is tickling our sister to share the Kahlua.

I'll show you, I think silently, clenching my hands and crumbling the paper. I realize then that I am just like my father. I go to my bed in a cold sweat of terror.

The next morning, the magical mask is cockeyed on the counter. A pair of gloves, red and black, almost sinister, yet powerful, tucked beneath the magical mask.

At lunch, our father returns to his chair, his knuckles tattooed and holding a bag full of money. I skip out of lunch and buy a red and black cape from the costume store.

As the Kahlua comes out and I go to tuck the cape under the magical mask with the gloves, I see already a pair of red boots with black laces and streaks that light up.

—

Under cover of night, when we siblings are not drunk enough and considering more, we go to the phone and see it has all disappeared: the cape, the boots, the gloves, the magical mask, and our rotten father.

We turn on the television and flip to the news.

'Heinous!'

'Diabolical!'

'Incomparably EVIL!'

Our father hovers above a burning building, his red and black cape fluttering handsomely in the wind. He stares into the camera.

We have healed him, our father. And now he is the world's concern, not mine.

"Dreadful was the din / Of hissing through the hall, thick-swarming now / With complicated monsters, head and tail." (Book X., lines 521 – 523.) Artist: Gustave Duré. Engraver: Louis Paul Pierre Dumont. From *Paradise Lost* by John Milton. New York: Collier, n.d. [ca. 1880?]

THE TOWN THAT BANNED FUN

Ben Crowley

When it became exceptionally dark, our fathers dragged us out. The river was raging. Our fathers dragged us to the river as we banged our hands on their hands. They dragged us by our ankles, ruining our jeans in the grass and the dirt. They dragged us because we were going to witness something.

They stood us there, our fathers, behind us with their hands on our shoulders. It was like they were a wall, and we faced a firing squad.

A long row of terror-stricken reflections was asleep along the riverbank in the black water. We were directed to keep our eyes on the bridge. A half dozen men without children gathered on it. It was as if they would step up to the edge and hurl themselves in.

I trembled and tried to touch the hands of either boy on either side of me. The grass between my feet was flat where I had stepped and smelled of mud.

The river was so black in the middle of the night. I could see only slivers of movement. It was as if it were not a river but a great gash rending the universe. My father squeezed me, and I saw that the men held large bags on the bridge.

They flicked on flashlights and held their black bags high above their heads. The flashlights made the bags glow as if they were pregnant with things from other worlds.

We have wasted so much time, they said. Things are going to be different.

It was as if the voice of a god had come through a cloud and now rested on the river as if the words did not move through time but now permeated all space and all time. They lowered their bags, their lights jumping oddly in different directions. Again, it was as if they were undoing time.

The contents of their bag, as they spilled, some of it drifted, some of it moved forward through the air before floating down, then all, as if lighter than water, tumbled over the river. None of them sank.

The thousands upon thousands of shapes glowed bright in the beams of their flashlights. Imagine my horror as my father's hands squeezed my shoulders as if I were the handle of a shovel because I had seen a balloon animal in one circle of light—pink, a rabbit, hand-folded and see-through.

There was no width of the river without them; they filled it end to end, some even crowding up to the bank as if, in the rush of the river, nudging their noses or ears up at our feet, as if reaching out for anyone. But we stuck there like sand as the river filled with color. It is eerie, the glow a balloon has in the dark.

As they filled above the river, moved along by wind and water, the pinks, yellows, and greens were so bright in the darkness that they would never disappear. But this river took things out of space, out of time. So black was this river's tail that in the end, even the brightest blue monkey, with extra balloons bent to wear like a hat— though still glowing like a solid blue star as the pink parrots and orange roses blinked out around it—even this happy, blue monkey was finally swallowed.

And so went all the insides of the sonless men's big black bags. And so, the men stepped down from the bridge and clicked off their flashlights. And the river became nothing more than a gash as if nothing of any wonder had ever passed through it. Now our fathers patted our shoulders.

We were then taken back to our houses. Our blankets were all that were left. But so many were replaced if the characters could not be unstitched. I slept under a mountain of suitable grey now. I cannot even remember what characters I slept under before, so depleted is my memory, my memory of fun. Now all that was left of our rooms, four scoured walls, a floor, and a ceiling, so empty except for a desk.

———

The first changes came in short bursts.

Emily, a girl with a sour face, was tied by the wrist to her mother so they could only get an arm's width apart. Whenever Emily struggled, her mother yanked, and sometimes so hard she made herself fall over too. Emily's mother pulled Emily through the grass early one morning when the sky was nearly white. In her hand, which she held out as if leading the way, Emily's mother clutched a small cotton clown with red hair and a ball nose. The doll's name was Cooky, Cooky the Clown.

Emily slipped to her knees, where wet soil began taking on sand. A robin landed in a tree. She had known Cooky since she was eleven months old. Her mother yanked her up, and they trudged to the river. When her mother knelt by the river, she yanked Emily forward. She yanked Emily to ensure she did not escape the river, which Emily tried.

She felt Cooky under her thumb. She did not want to make this so gruesome, but Emily was pulling and straining her shoulder. She submerged the doll in the water and pressed down with the heel of her palm. She held it there as if drowning a rabbit, as the doll soaked in the water.

Emily cried and beat her mother. She hit her mother with her arms like they were clubs. Her mother held the doll down under the water until the doll and the river were equally heavy, and then she let go. The doll turned over and was quickly taken by the river. Emily continued beating her mother until her mother stood up and again was three times as tall.

———

It was a young boy's birthday who was having a terrible life. He was inside, in the dark, peeking from under the corner of cardboard and comforter, which his mother had respectively taped and pinned to the windows. It was 3 am, and his mother still had not finished burning the piles and piles.

His mother glowed in the firelight and obscured in the smoke. She had been tending the fire since five in the evening, creating cracking, popping, and smoke. But no one complained because she had taken on so much of her neighbors' burdens box by box.

The boxes burned strangely, as many were full of plastic, metal, cotton, or nylon. Some popped in great bangs, and the boy's mother would duck down. Some smothered the fire, so she rekindled it, dragging in sizable branches quickly caught in the heat.

The neighborhood sufficiently blackened in hazardous smoke, and nothing could be smelled save for the pounds and pounds of smoldering plastic. The boy's mother crept in through the door and felt her way to the kitchen. There was no timer, no risk of alarm.

Tending the fire, she had counted every last one of the one-thousand eight-hundred seconds in her head. She breathed deep and coughed. Even inside her house, there was only the smell of the fire. She opened the oven and slid out the cake. She would not risk cooling it; she would not risk frosting it. She left it in the pan, stuck and lit a candle in the center, and carried it by tea towel over to the table. There her son sat, as still as the night.

She rechecked the windows to be sure no light could escape, then slid out the paper she had stuffed in a joint under the table. She unfolded it, and she and her son held it together.

They did not dare even mouth it for fear of the involuntary mechanics of their mouths letting slip any joy, any single word. They imagined the sounds of each word, keeping their mouths shut so tight it was as if they were glued. *Happy birthday to you. Happy birthday dear--*

Then the boy blew out his candle.

He was today seven years old. Gifts indeed — though today his mother had undoubtedly in the boxes held fire trucks, squirt guns, army men, rocket ships — were an impossibility.

The fire outside clicked out as suddenly as an electric light. But their windows were so thoroughly blacked out, not the light change they noticed, but the deep thudding sounds of boots breaking down sticks. It did not matter that she had covered the windows with blankets. They were easily broken.

For a birthday wish, mother and son have not been seen since, and their house has remained gapingly empty.

———

It had started on a night at the bowling alley when we registered our names. At first, the power was cut. All we heard was the whirring of reset machines and the half dozen balls flying back underground, and the bang of one ball dropped out of fear.

There was no warning, only the rush of what felt like thousands of bodies, the screaming, the shoving.

Making it out, you were then read your rights. We had thought it was nothing when the clowns were all arrested. It was very early summer, that late hour in the summer, when the sprinklers came on the second time, and the kids sat down for dinner. They came in very regular cars. There was no uniformity about it. They dressed in very regular clothes and, I don't know how to say it, but I think it was the seriousness in their faces.

The clowns answered their doors and stood there with their oversized shoes, readying to squeeze their water-shooting flowers. They had spent a lifetime in makeup. They had everyday worn the wig and nose. But now they were yanked out like teeth stuffed into cars. They were rubbed with sheets soaked in alcohol, stuttering and straining for answers. The clowns' noses were plucked and stuffed in dark bags. The clowns leaned on against the windows as they were driven away.

From our cars, radios were yanked from dashboards—for still moments singing as do chickens made headless and running for fear—and beaten savagely with baseball bats on the street. Baseball bats were acceptable now because all balls, gloves, and caps were crushed and compacted into dense blocks of trash.

Men in green masks with eye holes brought bolt cutters to swing sets. They took the footballs and beach balls and popped them with knives.

The dogs and the cats were all run out of town.

The candy store was burned down.

There was nothing to save us but the magician. But the magician was so old that, when they pulled up behind him in seven black vans, it was easy to strip him of his robes and break his staff and convince him quickly, in his deep senility, that he had never been a wise magician at all, but a skilled and happy salesman.

When the magician, with an armful of printers, arrived at the door of a painter, the painter reached behind the magician's ear and pulled out a coin. At that moment, the coin held between them, and the two desperate men began to shiver with hope.

Le Suicide. "Suicide." Artist: Félix Vallotton. From *Félix Vallotton;
Biographie* by Julius Meier-Graefe. Berlin, Paris: Edmond Sagot, J. A.
Stargardt [1898]

Toute la ville semblait me regarder avec des yeux de spectre. Les fenêtres des maisons blanches étaient des orbites vides dans des crânes, et mon imagination m'entourait de mille ennemis silencieux. "London about me gazed at me spectrally. The windows in the white houses were like the eye sockets of skulls. About me my imagination found a thousand noiseless enemies moving." Artist: Henrique Alvim Corrêa.

From *La Guerre des Mondes* by Herbert George Wells. Brussels: L. Vandamme & Co. [1906]

The Cabinet of Children

In the first two issues of *Maev Barba Presents*, we publish the first four chapters of *The Cabinet of Children* by Bob Selcrosse.

This first chapter details Bob's attachment to Long Beach, Washington, where Bob grew up and where *The Cabinet of Children* takes place. In the second chapter, Bob visits a palm reader.

LONG BEACH, WASHINGTON

Bob Selcrosse

The following image is of two planetary bodies, one in orbit around the other:

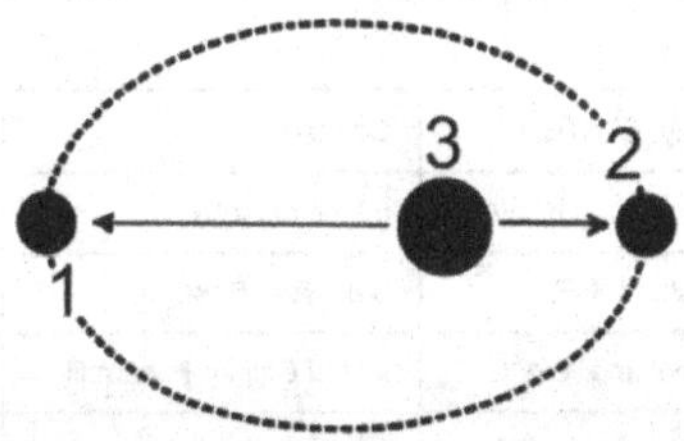

The apsides refer to the farthest (1) and nearest (2) points reached by an orbiting planetary body (1 and 2) concerning a primary or host body (3). The line of apsides is the line connecting positions 1 and 2. Source: https://en.wikipedia.org/wiki/Apsis

Positions 1 and 2 are two different positions of the same orbiting body. Position 1 is when it's furthest from the massive body, the apoapsis. Position 2 is when it's closest to the massive body, the apsis.

In this way, an orbiting body, even when force or will sends it farther and farther away, as far as it can go, the more massive body reins it in, and the circles become smaller and smaller.

The orbiting body's ability to distinguish itself from the massive body, the host body, as it grows closer, then further, then closer again, becomes more impossible and necessary.

If you are the orbiting body, your host body defines your every movement, no matter where you think you are going.

A list of my past residences and employers:

	City, STATE	Company	Distance from LB (in miles)
0.	Long Beach, WA	(place of birth)	0
1.	Astoria, OR	Selcrosse Books	19.1
2.	Spokane, WA	Inland Empire Papermill	429.6
3.	Hood River, OR	(cousin's house)	196.3
4.	Wallua, WA	Packaging Corp. of America	322
5.	Tacoma, WA	Benston Printing	140.7
6.	Moses Lake, WA	A&H Printing	328.1
7.	Olympia, WA	Weyerhauser Log Yard	111.4
8.	Yakima, WA	Yakima Papermill	240.2
9.	Oysterville, WA	Oysterville Sea Farms	14.6
10.	Astoria, OR	Selcrosse Books	5.5
11.	Long Beach, WA	(Eric Thralby)	0

It took eleven moves: Long Beach -> Long Beach. Everything in between, my so-called "life," looks accidental now, like a long series of diminishing steps.

The idea that we can never come back home is a farce. No matter where I went, I was doomed to return.

A war between my willpower and the gravity of Long Beach. Fate has drawn me back, reeled me in, Long Beach has clutched me to her bosom and pushed my head under the sand, sinister geography. I feel tight in my chest, even now. I am like a sausage on a string.

I felt it first at Inland Empire, my first job at eighteen. My fate came to life. It became a man under my bed. It became a subway in a tunnel. Something pulled me around each corner. When I was young, it visited me in the bathroom. Something, the shadow of a man behind the shower curtain, waiting. Now it is an ever-present rock pressing down on my chest.

As you can see on the map, my life as Bob Selcrosse is a series of concentric circles, tightening and tightening around Long Beach, Washington.

The Inland Empire papermill is a massive network of impossible machines. It is like a rusting space station, self-contained, gargantuan, and scraping the planet into its mouth.

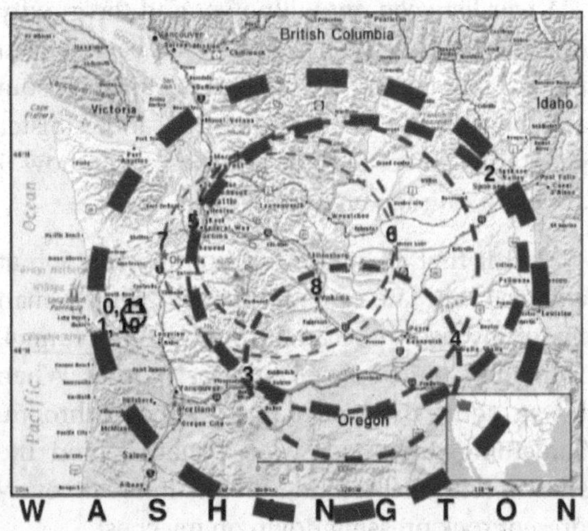

Map - This map has my past addresses numbered with circles added, illustrating the initial expansion and the following contraction. Original map image retrieved from: https://ian.macky.net/pat/map/us/wa/wa.html

The facilities at Inland Empire are arranged by process. Hence, at one end, the log trucks come in from the forest with beds full of felled trees which are hoisted up by one machine, stripped by another, shaved, and sliced into 2x4s by another, or munched and crushed and churned into pulp by another. From fresh logs to printer paper, the Inland Empire facilities stretch as long as four football fields laid out end to end. It is a hyper-efficient network of paper production, like a giant god whose sole purpose is to consume the forest, a giant lying on its side and reaching out and dragging in swaths and swaths of forest. The day I saw all its buzzing, trembling parts, I thought, 'It's true, we've made a god, and now we've stuffed him in this warehouse.'

You could hear the fir trees banging in from the trucks and tumbling through these machines as big as city blocks, many of these firs nearly the height of the Space Needle.

It was like living in an apartment building where every floor is comprised of active construction sites, or like living inside an alien ship that is always at task repairing or expanding itself, or living in the abandoned housing projects of China where ratcheting, hammering, sawing goes forever on and on from every direction on every floor, for only the one lone family — living in only one apartment of thirty-two floors worth — alone to hear. You could not escape these sounds. Trees can smash houses. Trees can raze whole rows of offices. The trees are like thunder coming out of your head.

I was good at my job and tasked to work the machine we called 'Stargate.'

I climbed up to the top and investigated its teeth. This was routine. You checked the beast's teeth to find branches, stakes, or fencing — anything that could get stuck and keep it from chomping. In the event of a halt, we turned it off. Typically, you turned it off, spotted the thorn, and then plucked it. Conceptually, it was an easy machine. Per the event in question, however, I could see nothing. I called my supervisor.

"See anything inside it?" I asked him.

We scratched under our hard hats and looked down in there. It was like skydiving into a city of skyscrapers. My supervisor had gum issues and routinely pressed his fingers above his teeth to check for density, sometimes reaching back to massage his molars. He always looked in pain, doing this. Finally, he removed his fingers and wiped them off against his pants. "Nothing," he said.

"Me neither," I said.

"I want to try again," he said. "While it's moving." He made a circle with his finger and pointed at me, then at the controls. I fired it up.

The power came on, and the sound returned. It sounded like the handle of a locked door. I followed the sound and saw two teeth weren't meeting but scraping.

The machine remained off. After three days, we lowered maintenance specialists in like spelunkers.

"I like it," said my supervisor. We leaned over the edge of the machine and watched three men descend into its mouth, their headlights pitching back and forth as they looked around. "We run The God, but these guys fix it." He played with his fingers so they bent and snapped back on the metal edge, their impact dribbling tiny echoes down the machine's throat. "I understand you don't want to be here very long," he said. He smelled like beef and bread.

Something clanged in the machine.

I blinked. His head looked three times its size in shadow. "No," I said. "I mean. I don't make plans," I said. "I might stay or go. I don't know."

"We are the greatest papermill in the Pacific Northwest. We touch it all." He drummed his fingers. "Every single mail slot. Fifty percent of all textbooks in Oregon and Washington are printed on Inland paper. We are in the minds of children. We are notices from Death." He massaged his gums and then looked at the results on his fingers. "We are the receipt paper for chewing gum."

———————————

He was a fine man. And I liked the job. But eventually, my orbit sent me away again. I came to stay with my cousin Amber in Hood River and then moved on to Benston Printing in Tacoma, Washington, after a brief stint at the packing job in Wallua. I got away again, 328.1 miles from Long Beach to Moses Lake. It was not as far away as Spokane, but it was something.

At A&H, I learned to work the printing press. There are many things to touch and turn, and sending paper through its ink became a living process. It was like massaging a pregnant cat, delivering its babies. Only your fingers did not pull away full of blood but of ink.

I was working the press, pushing it, pulling it, operating it as required, then finding that it became more and more like a body. In my mind, it appeared not as a machine but as a fleshy giant lying on its side, its long spindly handles sticking straight up like the legs of an ancient and giant grasshopper.

One day, as I operated, bent, twisted, and pulled the machine, the ink began to pour as if it had been wounded. I could not find its source. It pooled at my feet.

It was after hours. I was alone. No one could see what I had done. When the ink had run out, I mopped it up. I mopped the floor three times and scoured it with bleach.

It was nothing. I had overfilled the ink block. It was the lull of the machine. The sound of the machine, its every clinking, shifting piece.

It was a living creature I put energy into. I moved its body. I pushed its arms. I gave it life. After I mopped, it no longer resembled a machine but a creature hugging tightly to its legs. I had wounded it, and now it lay there consoling itself.

———

I grew up a failure and have remained a failure. I have held more than thirty jobs.

In 2011, I took a job in Oysterville to help my mother.

Oysterville is along **Willapa Bay** on the **Long Beach Peninsula** in **Pacific County, Washington**, United States. It is approximately 5 miles (8.0 km) from the city and 15 miles (24 km) from **Long Beach**. Founded in 1841 as an oyster fishing village, the community is registered on the **National Register of Historic Places** as the Oysterville Historic District. It currently has a population of about 20 residents.

Source: https://en.wikipedia.org/wiki/Oysterville,_Washington

I put tourists in a boat and took them on the water. I slapped bread with oysters at the Oysterville Sea Farms.

My mother was dreaming again. I took over the bookstore in Astoria. Selcrosse Books. By day, I worked at the farms. And by night, I ran my mother's receipts and helped her to bed.

We did not allow cell phones in the store. We used only candlelight. It was the draw of the place. A bookstore without the comforts of the modern century. No air conditioning, no electrical lighting, and only an in-store telephone. And even that, my mother had tried many ways to get rid of it. But I needed to get in touch with her. Her customers needed to get in touch with her. The in-store telephone was non-negotiable, so she kept it, though she remained somewhat ashamed. While I was sitting down to read through a cracker-thin stack of receipts one night, the in-store telephone rang. My mother, beside the window watching the rain, picked it up at the second ring.

"Hello," she said.

I listened closely and did not move, but under the sound of the rain, I couldn't hear anything from the other line.

"No," she said. "We don't carry that."

"Don't carry what?" I said. She was hardly aware of her stock. She haunted the bookstore with what habits she knew but had no spirit left to keep it afloat.

"I'm sorry," she said. "We don't have it." She hung up the phone. "Something about cabinet repair."

"Cabinet repair?" I said.

She continued to watch the rain, her fingers on the phone. "I'm going to bed," she said.

It had rained for three days.

Rain put me to sleep. That was the nature of it. It put me to sleep, so I dreamt of nothing and almost woke for nothing. Rain was my surest aid in sleep, and I wanted it every night. I woke up the night of the phone call. My mother left a candle on.

We slept upstairs. I don't know if I mentioned that. We slept upstairs and ran the bookstore below. When I came downstairs, I saw my mother in the candlelight. She stood amidst the books, the candle on the desk. I stopped mid-step and held my weight on the stair rail. "Mom?" I said.

She had a pile of books in her arms. She rushed. She was old, but there was a rushed anxiety to her movement. She lugged the books from one shelf to another and pulled on spine after spine, shoving most of them back in with the others but pulling the odd one out and piling it up. She had gathered nearly a dozen books, all of them hardcover.

"Mom," I said. I took them away. Her arms shook.

"Bob," she said.

"It's two in the morning," I said.

She looked out the window. It was black outside. She nodded. I helped her upstairs. Only then did I remember the candle. I returned, blew it out, and looked at the books.

Kim

The Grey Fairy Book

The Wonderful Wizard of Oz

All classic kids' books. I reshelved them and then went to bed.

The second night it happened again, only this time it wasn't the candle, but the thick black smoke that woke me up.

My mother was asleep, standing over a trashcan full of fire, burning pages from *The Railway Children*.

"Stealing." Artist: Louis Rhead. From *The Life and Death of Mr. Badman* by John Bunyan. New York: R.H. Russell [1900]

THE PALMIST

Bob Selcrosse

Whenever the impulse flaming comes—to burn up houses or blow the Ferris wheelbase and send it rolling over children—I slip on my special disguise and sneak into the fish market under the bridge.

The Astoria-Megler Market is a midnight market as wet as the ocean itself, an under-bridge fish market that is not only leaked on by rain slipping through the bridge but lapped at by the river reaching up the concrete on which the market rests. Leaks from each stand turn into streams and extend into long puddles pooling at grates, positioned at various areas over the concrete and down the mud into the ocean. It is a place of puddles, freshwater, and saltwater, which are as wet as a fish. Again, it is a wet market full of trembling fish, thrashing the walls of their watery tanks.

There is every kind of fish imaginable in this market, and this is why its enthusiasts wear high collars over their necks and hats low over their eyes. There is something obscene about it, all the squirming, the wetness, the dark. I poke my fingers in the fish tanks. It is a place as dark as the internet.

The wet market is made of rows of awnings in various states of decay. Some bent down, some molding. By day it is respectable; tough old customers hock their oysters and mussels, and old women suck cigars and decapitate fish. But every night at about nine o'clock, the place switches; all the lights go off save for the center tank light and the light of the fortune teller. Now emerge from black night: enthusiasts of the horrors of fish.

We gathered shoulder-to-shoulder, scrambling around the glass aquarium under the remaining lightbulb. I am here for one lightbulb in particular, a way behind my back, a special lightbulb, a soft pink lightbulb that should be easy to forget. For now, again, in true Selcrosse fashion, I am here at first to distract myself from fate and instead lose myself in these unfathomable nightmares.

The tank to my left calls to me. The man is a sailor with a red mustache and yellow teeth. A train of seven cars rattles above our heads and drops a curtain of rain between us. I step over it and head to the man.

We stooped to look inside the tank, obscured in black like a volcanic dust storm. The sailor was so close to me that I could hear his lip hair bristle as he spoke. "Caught her at the very last minute. I was about to throw in the towel. A whole day and no creatures but trout. Then I saw her reach the surface with her big, beautiful hands, like a prom girl ready for the dance."

"I don't see it," I said.

Something like a ghostly hand passed before our faces.

"Isn't she beautiful," he said.

Then I saw her. She had released her ink, and now was a twist of limbs in a water-trapped fog made of blackness and the glint of thick white limbs sucking the glass. As the limbs slid down, one after the other, like a bed of snakes retreating, or a white forearm sliding over a nose, the squid revealed its eye. It was as large as a baseball. Its skin's translucent whiteness was a divine light in the black of its water.

I stammered. "How much?"

I felt the man's moisture in my ear. "Seven hundred."

I had to leave the man. For me, that is a substantial amount of money.

Dallying about the market, I traced my fingers along the other tanks, waiting for any of the other owners to look away. I was here for the fish in their water, not for their owners breathing on my neck.

I found an angler, its smile like a human's but with a slightly larger mouth. We made eye contact like a man who had lost touch with his soul.

I found an untended, unlighted tank on a truck-pulled trailer full of vampire squid, their bodies pulsing in and out of darkness like heads attached to cloaks.

I climbed onto the trailer and stared into the tank. I wanted to put my hand in. Seeing them from above, they seemed like harmless jellyfish. If I squinted, they looked like rain clouds. A vampire squid has a webbing of skin that connects its eight arms, making the squid's underbelly like a vampire's cloak.

There is a nervous energy behind me. I could sense it in the heat like a fire had come on. I knew. I knew without a doubt, by the heat in my neck and the weight in my gums, that now was the time for the bidding.

A few flashlights are held by Astorian men surrounding a relatively small cage, about the size of a small car's trunk.

The bidding began, and the fish will be sold tonight or kept and reported tomorrow morning to the Astoria fish and wildlife authorities. Any offer higher than the fine for illegally selling the fish will be accepted.

Sometimes an offer lower will be accepted. Sometimes there is pressure from the others. If you do not give them the deal, they will sell you under if they do not expect you to produce more miraculous fish within the month.

I squeeze around the lighted tank with my other shoulders. There is nothing there but sand. It is an empty tank. But then I see it is a stargazer, the uncanniest of fish. It looks exactly like a face sticking up from the ground, like a man cursed to live at the bottom of the ocean. It burrows underneath the sand so that only its eyes and mouth remain, its mouth like a zipper unzipped in the earth, and its eyes, lidless, never closing.

At the starting bid of one thousand dollars, I slipped from the shoulders and turned to face the pink light.

The palmist was set up beside the tremendous concrete support which holds up the curving overpass. She sits outside by the dry goods tables, which I can see by the faint light of the palmist's pink bulb.

"Inhabitants of the Sea." Artist: Alphones de Neuville. Engraver: Henri Théophile Hildibrand. From Vingt Mille Lieues sous les Mers by Jules Verne. Paris: Hetzel, n.d. [1871?]

She was in all black in front of her black booth, sunken and wrinkled, eyes perpetually open. She was a shroud of black: black robes, hair, thick black earrings, heavy black necklace, nails, and teeth. It was as if only her mouth and eyes were visible, her eyes, eyes that looked so far into the future that she too seemed like the stargazer, gazing up at me, her body covered underneath the very bottom of the ocean. She knew instinctively what I wanted. Without greeting me or even looking me in the eye, she shoved her black curtain open and stood waiting.

I slipped into the curtains as if diving into a sail and quickly closed them all behind me. We were in almost complete darkness, the only lingering pink light outside.

Inside the black, she was ample like squid in tight clothing. The fat black of her clothing mixed in with her curtains and her entire surroundings, and I, too, felt as if I were inside her dress or if the entire booth was made from her body.

She struck a match and lit a candle. Her eyes gleamed from thick flesh. She leaned forward and slid my hand in her fingers as if we were engaging in sex. "You are Bob Selcrosse," she said.

"Yes," I said. "We have met before."

"Yes, well," she said. She pressed her thumbs in on my palm. "You have a twin."

"No."

"A brother?"

"No, no siblings at all."

She pressed my hands in a way that made me feel as powerless as a child. "You have a broken headline. Are you a thinker?"

My phone rang. I switched it to silent through my pants. "No," I said. "Not really."

She ran her index finger down the center of my hand as if it were supposed to react like a fish. "You were hospitalized."

I took my eyes off her sweaty lips and looked at my hand. She was pointing at the fate line, not the lifeline. I pointed each out. "Fate. Life. Heart line. Headline"

She looked at me, then looked at my hand, then at me. "You are prone to many changes in life from external forces."

"Everyone's been to the goddamn hospital," I said.

There was a scuffle outside, likely some fun with the squid. The sound of the ocean lapping up concrete did not diminish, and the pink light buzzed above our heads.

"You will meet someone," she said. Her eyes flashed up at mine. They were eyes like the sheen in a milky, shallow, white decorative plate. "A long-lost brother, I think."

"No," I said. "I don't think so."

"He is much older than you. He's old enough to be your father."

My phone rang again. Even on vibrate, it was loud.

"Who is calling you?" she said.

I left it in my pocket.

"You ought to pick it up," she said.

I waved away the suggestion.

"Look," I said. "It doesn't matter. Please continue. I'm sorry. It was a stupid interruption."

It rang again.

Unable to take it out of my right pocket with my left hand, I took my hand away from the fortune teller and took the phone from my pocket. I didn't know the number. I answered and only held the receiver to my mouth. "Stop calling me,"

I said, then slid the phone back into my pocket. I gave the woman my hands and said, "There, no more interruptions."

She quickly took both hands again and slowly moved them up my wrists as she spoke. "You have nothing and have achieved nothing.

"You have sacrificed all society for yourself," she said. "Yes, you will meet a man. I see that. He is alive, that is sure. Are you able to call him on the phone?" She looked up hopefully, the obscene nubile youngness that glows from a grotesque lecherous old woman.

I snatched away my hands and thrust her money. Gazing one last time into her black room of curtains, I felt her face fade away as if burrowing under the darkness. Yet still from the darkness, her eyes flashed and glowed, her unclosing eyes and her zipper-like mouth.

My phone rang again, and I walked away into the night market as the vendors packed up.

I stood by a puddle from the ocean and answered my phone.

The voice on the other end was Eric Thralby.

"I- I think I've found him."

We agreed to meet. Midweek. Noon. On Sid Snyder Drive.

"She lighted a new match. Then she sat under a beautiful Christmas tree, with thousands of candles burning upon the green branches." Artist: Hans Tegner. From *Fairy Tales and Stories* by Hans Christian Andersen. New York: The Century Co. [1900]

"He threw himself into the water and began to swim." Artist:
Carlo Chiostri. From *Le Avventure di Pinocchio* by Carlo Collodi.
Florence: R. Bemporad & Figlio, n.d. [1902]

ILLUSTRATIONS

All illustrations in this issue of MBP are in the public domain and were sourced from oldbookillustrations.com

Before the first chapter of The Cabinet of Children, the frontispiece was originally captioned, "It was the demon Beelzebub, whom he had called up." The artist is John Dickson Batten. It was published in *English Folk and Fairy Tales* written by Joseph Jacobs. New York: G.P. Putnam's Sons, n.d.

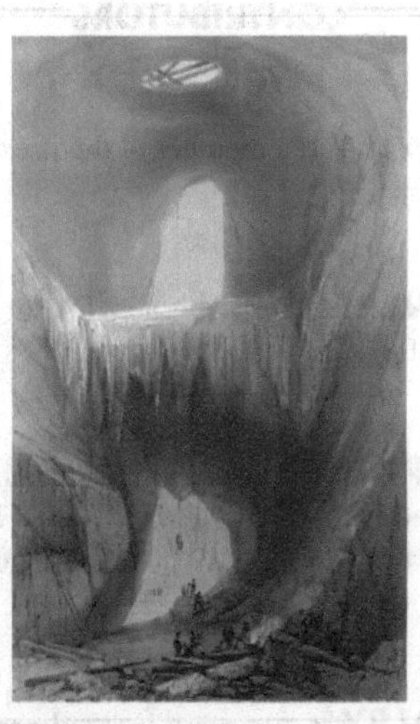

Intérieur des mines de fer de Danemora [sic]. "Interior of the iron mine at Dannemora." Artist: Mayer, Auguste Etienne François. From *Voyages en Scandinavie, en Laponi, au Spitzberg et aux Feröe (Atlas, vol. 2)* under the direction of Paul Gaimard.

PREVIOUS PUBLICATIONS

"Dead Horses" was originally published in Fiction Southwest.

All other stories were originally published in Deep Overstock.

CONTRIBUTORS

BEN CROWLEY is a member of the Bremerton Writers Society.

ROBERT EVERSMANN is an editor at *Deep Overstock* and an intern for *Maev Barba Presents*.

BOB SELCROSSE is a long-time and faithful (aside from all the betrayals) friend of Maev Barba. He is happy to be in the writer's group and still be published among friends.

ERIC THRALBY is a captain by trade and works wood on his long off days. He time-to-time pilots the Bremerton Ferry (Bremerton—Vashon; Vashon—Bremerton), while other times sells books on amazon.com. He'll sell any books the people love, strolling down to library and yard sales, but he loves especially books of Romantic fiction, not of risqué gargoyles, not harlequin romance, but knights, errant or of the Table. He has published work in Deep Overstock and read at local readings at the Gig Harbor Candy Company and the Lavender Inne, also in Gig Harbor.

MAEV BARBA is the editor of *Maev Barba Presents*.

Maev Barba
Presents

Maev Barba Presents
Published by Pluto House
www.plutohouse.space

Cover art by Lucas (bobsokova)